Tips For Your Last Year on Earth

Tips For Your Last Year on Earth

Written by Tara Jean O'Brien

illustrated by Richard Warren

Published by Vulpine Press in the United Kingdom in 2023

ISBN: 978-1-83919-452-8

Illustrations by Richard Warren

www.vulpine-press.com

Tara would like to dedicate this book to the most patient husband in the world, Art.

Rich would like to dedicate this work to his two candles in the darkness, Freddi and Billie.

Hey!

HEY, YOU!

Yeah, YOU, scumbag!

What if you found out this was your last year on Earth? Would you really keep trying to make the world a "better place"? Of course not! Stop pretending to have a moral compass and be honest. You'd shove burritos and Big Mac's in your gob like a pig in shit and destroy more souls than a Kardashian.

(Better make that sex tape while you still can!)

In case you don't have a television, Twitter account, or a pulse: the end of the world IS nigh. This really is YOUR last year on Earth. No ifs, ands, or buts. Game over, chump.

(Quit wasting time and bring on the drugs!)

One quick thing before you bust into the diabetes-inducing goodness that is the meat of this book. We do NOT suggest that you live each day like it's your last. No. That's trash advice. If today were your last day on Earth, you wouldn't get to finish the rest of the ice cream, bang your sister-in-law, or cut your boss's brake lines. There's plenty left to destroy that can't all be completed in a single day. Hence the creation of this fabulous compendium of tips!

Thanks for taking this journey with us.

Go get 'em, dickhead!

Tara Jean & Rich

Ignore red lights. They're the only things preventing you from reaching your full potential.

Eat expired foods. Neither dates nor food should be the boss of you.

Tell kids the truth. Start with "there's no Santa," move on to who their real father is, and finally, explain why their face makes them so unattractive. Children aren't the future when there is no future.

Get a tattoo on your face. Nothing says, "No Regrets" like a tattoo on your face that says, "No Regrets."

Shave nothing. Every lover loves the gift of...surprise.

Visit old folks' homes. Hold their hands and tell the seniors how happy you are...that you'll never know how it feels to be that old.

Fill your yard with political signs. How else would the five people that live in your cul-de-sac know what you stood for?

Demand instant
gratification. Waiting is for
the weak.

Skydive without a parachute. The last thing that should hold you back is gravity.

Never do what you say you're going to do. Your aura of mystery will live on long after you do.

Buy a motorcycle. You'll want to leave physical evidence of how smart you were...by scattering your brain across the interstate.

Always place your shopping carts at an angle, in the middle of the aisle. Strangers will thank you for teaching them that time is just a construct.

Go to work when you're sick. Don't be the only person who never brought something in to share with the office.

Never seek inner peace.
Outer drunkenness is
cheaper.

Wear sunglasses indoors and at night. Disguising yourself as an idiot will stave off unwanted conversations.

Develop a food allergy. Don't let anyone take the easy way out after inviting you to dinner.

Be the loudest person in the room. It speaks volumes about who you are.

Spit in public. When the world doesn't feel like your oyster, make it look like one.

Try not to leave a tip. But if you do, make them wait for it.

Never drive electric vehicles. Innocent dinosaurs died so you could drive your child to school in an eight-passenger SUV.

Brag. Praise the things your friends can do...that you can do better.

Stake your reputation, and all your money, on your favorite sports team. When they lose, let your family pay for your mistakes.

Don't worry about your appearance. Maybe you were born with it; maybe you just got up late.

Start a podcast. It will free you from the burdens of having to maintain friendships.

Get plastic surgery. Do it because you want to, not because you have self-esteem issues that you can see right through your wet T-shirt.

Become an artist. Your parents don't have time to retire anyway.

Start a fad diet. Nothing should hold you back from reaching your goal of total weightlessness.

Talk to strangers. Share your favourite Bible verse with them.

Don't take drinks from strangers. The only thing you should be appropriating is other people's cultures.

Fly home no matter what the weather reports. Take the odds of dying in a plane crash over the odds of being seated next to racist Uncle Kirby and his pistol, "Pete," at Sunday dinner.

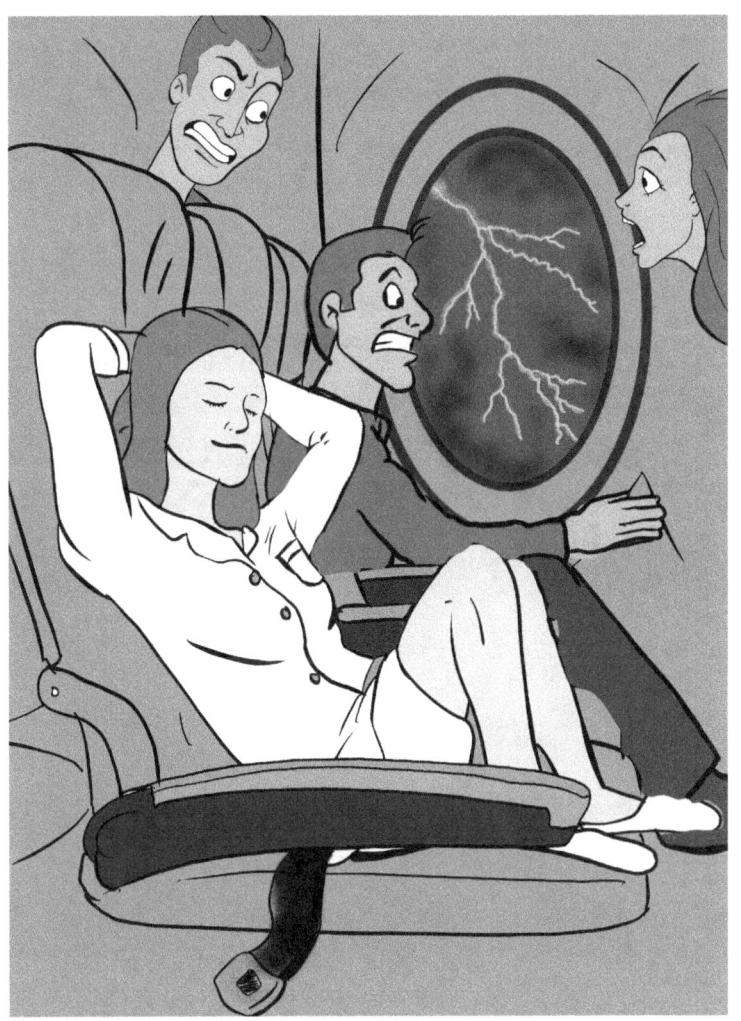

Wear an American flag bikini. Celebrate your independence from good taste.

Know when to walk away.
It's when the hot guy in
accounting has a good
view of your butt.

Don't donate your organs.

Not if your heart's not in it.

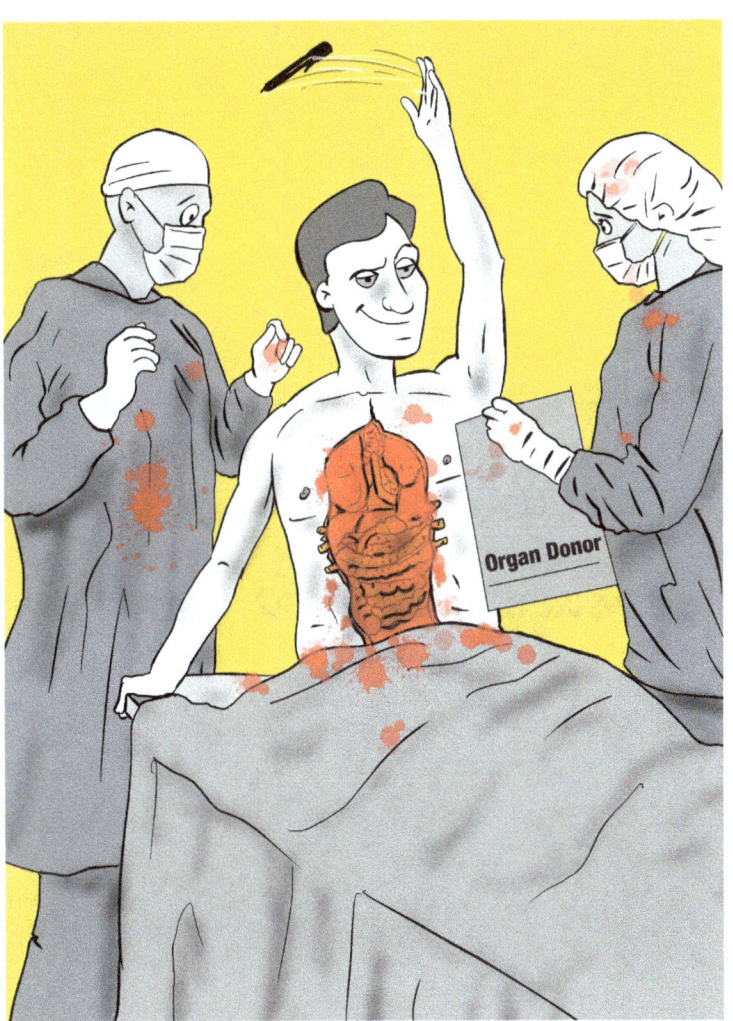

Learn about new cultures
so you know the best
ways to cancel them.

Reject all vegetables. The only thing you should be fuelled by is fossils.

Treat billionaires like an endangered species. Since there is only 1% of them, put them in cages and force them to mate.

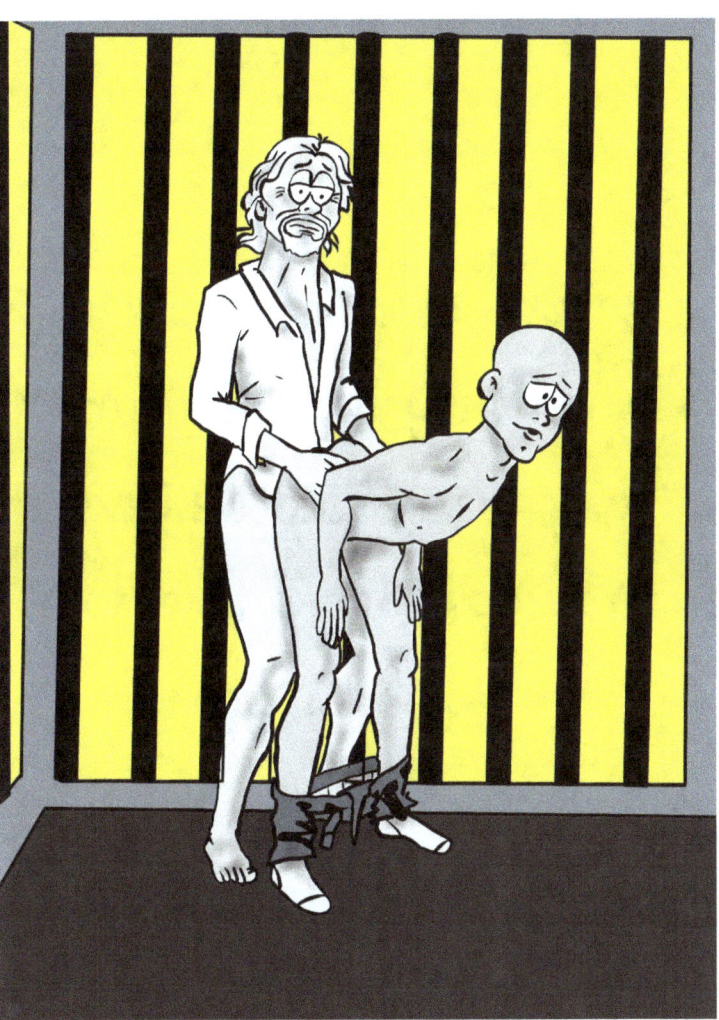

Believe older generations when they tell you you're lazy, weak, and entitled. You don't have time to prove them wrong.

Don't offer hope to poor people. Sell it to them.

Be like an alley cat. Stray all day, baby.

Fuck trees. Become a
paper terrorist.

Acknowledgements

We'd like to acknowledge the friends and family that have helped mould us into the deeply disturbed people we are today. An extra special thank you goes out to Troy Hewitt of Vulpine Press, who shepherded our worst instincts, and turned them up to 11.

About the author and illustrator

Tara Jean O'Brien is a graduate of the University of Southern California, and is a writer, actor, and comedian living in Los Angeles. You can stalk her on Twitter or Instagram at @tartarsauce1 or www.tarajeanobrien.com

Rich Warren is a graduate of Savannah College of Art and Design and works in a variety of art mediums. You can see more of his work @Oakmoonart on Instagram.